THE DINNER PARTY

AN EROTIC ADVENTURE

VICTORIA RUSH

VOLUME ONE

JADE'S EROTIC ADVENTURES - BOOK 1

COPYRIGHT

FEEL THE RUSH:

Jade's Erotic Adventures - Book 2

Jade discovers an exotic adventure club where strangers meet to explore each other's bodies in mysterious dark rooms. Using special effects to project swirling light patterns onto their figures, the shifting shadows provide just enough illumination to highlight their naked bodies while protecting their identities...

The Dark Room

Jade's Erotic Adventures - Book 3

Jade discovers a yoga club where members stretch and explore each other's bodies in the buff. She books an appointment, and during the first session meets a young redhead who tantalizes her with her flexibility and stunning body...

Naked Yoga

Jade's Erotic Adventures - Book 4

Jade goes on a nude cruise where naked couples enjoy unusual shipboard activities. On the first day she meets a stunning brunette who volunteers to show her around.

As they move from one exciting venue to another, Jade and her friend experience an escalating series of encounters with beautiful men and women, culminating in a final 'petit four' that takes everybody's breath away...

Nude Cruise

For the uninhibited...

1

HUNGER

It started innocently enough. After my passionless marriage dissolved, I resolved to push the boundaries of my boring love life. I'd jumped into wedlock with my college sweetheart at a young age, and neither of us had much prior sexual experience. Unless you count fully-clothed heavy petting with high school boys, which I think hardly qualifies.

Maybe it was my strict Pentecostal upbringing, which frowned upon any kind of sexual exploration before marriage. Or maybe it was my parents' frequent admonitions against all forms of sexual 'deviancy', including masturbation. Apparently, my husband had been equally repressed, because he never seemed to have much interest beyond quickies in the missionary position.

But I'd read enough steamy romance novels to realize there was a whole other world of sexual expression beyond boring monogamy. In spite of my frequent suggestions and gentle guidance, my husband never became adept at pleasing me. I was left to my own devices, alone with my romance novels, to find release.

When my husband eventually left me for another woman, I welcomed my newfound freedom. I dated with relish, jumping from one lover to another, even trying a few one-night stands. But no man seemed to have the spark that ignited my passion and imagination like my hunky literary heroes. So began my tentative and rapidly escalating online explorations to find sexual fulfillment.

I started with mainstream dating sites like Match.com then 'hook-up' sites like PlentyofFish and Craigslist—even AshleyMadison.com. Each forum presented more exciting prospects and more adventurous partners. I enjoyed getting in touch with my newfound sensuality and experimenting with new sexual practices.

But something was still missing. All the men I met ultimately just wanted the same thing—to get me into bed as quickly as possible and initiate contact in the typical manner, with the usual predictable ending. It was satisfying but somehow unfulfilling. I longed to find that truly transcendent experience that shattered my erotic expectations and left me completely spent, yet still wanting more.

One night, while trolling the usual online suspects, I tried typing something new into the search box: "transcendent erotic encounters". Amidst the usual litany of porn sites and massage parlors, I saw a listing near the bottom of the page that simply read *Fantasy Feast: Satisfy All Your Senses*.

Intrigued, I clicked on the link. A glowing website opened with a picture of beautiful men and women seated around a large dinner table wearing nothing but masquerade masks. Undeniable expressions of excitement and ecstasy adorned their faces.

Now *this* is something different, I thought. I clicked on

the site's *About* tab and held my breath as I read with increasing excitement about the club's service.

> *Fantasy Feast is a members-only club where patrons meet over a sumptuous five-star meal to explore and excite ALL their senses in an intimate and safe environment.*
>
> *We are very discriminating about who is accepted into our club, with only the most alluring and uninhibited invited to join. Upon qualification, you'll schedule an intimate dinner feast at our luxurious private villa.*
>
> *We prepare you for the meal with a full spa treatment, including sensuous bath, massage, and esthetic grooming. You'll be given a silk robe and slippers to don in preparation for the main event. We ask you to bring your own masquerade mask to wear at all times to protect your privacy and anonymity.*
>
> *You'll join a small group of pre-selected patrons at our elegant dining table in the main hall, where you'll be feted and serviced by our highly trained sensualists over four courses that will stimulate and excite all your senses: taste, sight, smell, sound—and touch.*
>
> *We guarantee you will not be disappointed. You can choose from a broad selection of a la carte services and waive any 'dishes' that are not to your liking. Upon completion of the feast, your senses will be excited beyond anything you've ever experienced and you will be satiated in every sense of the word.*
>
> *Call the private line below to begin your journey of discovery and fulfillment. We look forward to exciting your senses like they've never been before!*

The more I read, the more I could feel the heat build up between my legs. By the time I finished, I'd completely soaked my panties imagining myself seated at the Fantasy

Feast table watching my fellow dinner guests being 'serviced'—and being watched myself.

But there were so many questions. Exactly what kind of 'services' were offered? Who exactly did the servicing? Did the dinner guests engage each other directly, or did we remain passive in our chairs? Was everybody naked around the table, or wearing robes? And who were these 'sensualists'?

I was intrigued and excited in a way I'd never been before. I knew this was something I had to explore further. I reached for the phone and dialed the number.

2

HAUTE CUISINE

A woman with a sultry Scarlett Johansson voice answered on the second ring.

"Fantasy Feast. How may we satisfy you?"

Now *that* was a proposal I'd never heard phrased so perfectly before.

"I...was looking at your ad," I stammered. "I mean your *website*. I was wondering if I could talk with someone about your services. I've never tried anything like this before..."

Gawd, I thought. I sound like such a lightweight. They'll probably disqualify me even before I get through the front door.

"Not to worry," the Scarlett voice replied. "I completely understand. Our goal is your complete fulfillment. Was there something specific you wanted to ask about?"

She's not going to make this easy. Maybe that's all part of the game. I had to admit, the mystery and intrigue definitely added to the excitement.

"I was wondering about your 'a la carte' menu items. Can you clarify what this includes?"

"Of course," Scarlett replied. "Do you have our website open? Click on the Menu tab and you'll see our chef's selections for each course."

I clicked on the tab and scanned a mouth-watering list of dishes.

Chef's Menu:

First course: tomato gazpacho soup
Second course: arugula salad with baby beets
Third course: Chilean sea bass or filet mignon
Fourth course: chocolate mousse or crème brûlée

It certainly *looked* like a Michelin Star-worthy meal. But I was more interested in the *non-culinary* items on the menu. Had I somehow missed their intent?

"I sensed there were some—*other*—items on the menu," I probed. "Besides...*food*. Although the dishes do look delicious. I was looking for something *more*."

There was a momentary pause on the other end of the line.

"We wish to leave some of the *special* menu items to your imagination," Scarlett said. "We wouldn't want to shape your expectations or spoil the surprise. We engage *all* of your senses. I guarantee you will not be disappointed. We've never had a client ask for a refund."

I fully understood her reluctance to provide more specifics. This *was* after all a commercial enterprise that was operating on a precarious legal boundary. Promising sexual favors for money could get anyone in trouble with the law, and the woman couldn't be sure I wasn't the police fishing for ammunition to raid their premises.

But I was still a bit concerned about the line of *consent*. I wanted to be certain I'd be safe and able to say no if things got outside my comfort zone.

I paused, as I struggled to delicately express my concern.

"Will I have...*control* over the services at all times? I mean, will I be able to stop the activities, *the menu delivery*, if it's not to my tastes?"

"At all times," the woman assured. "Every patron will have a signaling device at their personal place setting that can be used to stop or return any menu item at any time."

Patron. I kind of liked the sound of that word. It sounded like I'd be the focus of their attention and that I'd be getting some very *special* attention.

That got me thinking about the *company* I'd have at the dinner table, and how far exactly our mutual 'engagement' might go.

"How many people attend each dinner event?" I asked. "What is the typical makeup in terms of age and gender?"

"Each dinner serves eight guests plus one hostess who orchestrates the service and facilitates engagement. This keeps the gathering suitably intimate and gives everyone a chance to get to know one another in a safe and comfortable environment. We ask each member to let us know their preferences in advance, then we carefully align the patrons and services for each event to ensure a stimulating mix of guests and activities. I think you'll find your dinner guests suitably arouse your interests."

I was already getting aroused just thinking of the possibilities. There was something appealing about the idea of pre-qualifying the people I'd be sharing intimate moments with and still having them be complete strangers. But I was still a little unclear with whom, and how, the erotic engagement would occur.

"What kind of engagement normally occurs between the guests?"

"During the actual dinner, it's limited to discussion only. And *watching*, of course. All of your senses will be engaged entirely from the privacy of your own seat at the table. After the final course is served, if you'd like to engage one or more patrons directly, you'll have the use of one of our private boudoirs for the remainder of the evening. This is included with our twenty-four-hour service."

"And we keep our masks on at all times to maintain our anonymity?"

"Yes. We ask every patron to wear a mask throughout the entire event. Just enough to veil your identity, but not so much to hide your facial expressions and beauty. I think you'll find most of the fun is in watching the expressions of our guests as they savor every stimulating course."

Wow. A five-star culinary experience at an intimate and upscale villa, with an exotic sampling of beautiful strangers. And complete anonymity. *I'm in.*

"I'm interested in attending one of your events," I said without hesitation. "What's the first step?"

"At the bottom of our home page you'll see a button labeled 'Profile,'" Scarlett said. "Just click on this to set up your personal profile, fill in your preferences, then select one of the available dates. We'll notify you when you've been accepted. Then pay the required deposit and arrive at our villa with a hungry appetite at the appointed time."

Everything about this operation screamed first-class professionalism. From the woman's voice on the phone, to the soft music playing on their website, to the vetting process of their customers. This was no cheesy escort service or massage parlor. I couldn't wait to get started.

"Thank you so much for your time and help," I said to Scarlett. "I'm looking forward to attending your feast!"

I hung up the phone and immediately clicked the Profile button.

TASTING MENU

The first field on the Profile page asked what anonymous profile name I'd like to use. I chose the exotic and sensuous-sounding name 'Jade'. I'd always loved that name, and now I had a chance to fulfill my fantasy of role-playing a mysterious Asian beauty. With my dark hair and high cheekbones, I might even be able to pull it off partially camouflaged under a masquerade mask.

The next field asked for my gender and gender-preferences. Men? *Check.* Women? I'd long-fantasized about having a tryst with a woman, and here was my chance. *Check.* Transgender? Maybe another day—this was already stretching my boundaries pretty far.

Next up was my age and age preferences. This is supposed to be a *fantasy*, right? As an attractive thirty-six-year-old woman with a well-exercised, nicely-toned body, I had nothing to be ashamed of. Nevertheless, I lied just enough to make me feel all the more desirable. I clicked the Age 25-35 box for myself and the 18-24 plus 25-35 boxes for my preferences.

Ethnicity? That might be tough to conceal, even under a

half-facemask. But that wouldn't stop me from imagining
myself any way I chose, once I got there. After some hesitation, I clicked the Caucasian box. Preferences? Asian—*check*.
African-American—*check*. My dream husband had been a
biracial African-Asian man with coffee-colored skin. I
always thought they produced the most beautiful children.
Curly brown hair with honey skin and doe eyes—absolutely
adorable. Caucasian? Fine—*check*. I suppose one or two in
the mix won't completely ruin it.

I scrolled down to the required payment fields where
there was a short note:

> *A deposit of five hundred dollars is required to schedule a face-
> to-face interview. Upon final acceptance, a second payment of
> five hundred dollars will secure your private membership. We
> accept PayPal only, to ensure your full anonymity.*

Five hundred bucks was substantial, but a five-star meal
and one night at a luxury hotel would easily cost that much.
This promised so much *more*.

I smiled as I clicked the 'Submit' button. *Submission*,
indeed. I was taking a giant leap into an unknown realm. I
felt a mix of nervous tension and release imagining myself
joining a mix of exotic strangers around the mysterious
fantasy table. Now it was just a matter of getting final
approval and scheduling the date.

My hand wandered unconsciously from the keyboard to
my inner thighs as I began to think about what erotic adventures lay in wait for me.

HORS D'OEUVRES

The next day, my heart skipped a beat when I logged onto the Fantasy Feast website and saw a notification in my inbox. I clicked on the message and read it with bated breath.

Congratulations on pre-qualification for membership to the Fantasy Feast club. The next step is to schedule a date to attend one of our dinner parties.

We'll complete the final qualification with a personal interview on the approved date. Please arrive three hours before the scheduled dinner time to complete the process and receive your personal spa preparation.

I clicked on the Schedule tab. It displayed a calendar for the current month with the first two weeks blacked out. I took this to be a good sign that they were popular enough to be booked up. I clicked on the first available Saturday, which pulled up a new window. An agenda displayed on the screen:

6:00 p.m. — Personal Interview
7:00 p.m. — Spa Treatment
8:00 p.m. — Final Preparation
9:00 p.m. — Dinner Party
11:00 p.m. — Guest Room Rendezvous (optional)

Submit

I loved the double meaning with the 'Submit' imagery, and I had to admit I found it a turn-on to click that button again. Those weren't the *only* buttons that were being pushed!

I was also a little intrigued by the cryptic agenda items 'Final Preparation' and 'Guest Room Rendezvous'. It was all so mysterious and exciting. My mind began to wander again imagining the surprises that awaited me as my legs parted and my erect nipples pressed against my silk blouse.

On the scheduled date, I could barely contain my excitement as I prepared for the mysterious event. I visited three costume shops before I found a masquerade mask that suited my style. I settled on a black lace eye mask that concealed enough of my face to disguise my identity, but still permitted my skin to breathe with comfortable facial movement. I didn't want any rough edges getting in the way of my—or anyone else's—pleasure. Thinking about all the things I could do in the guise of my fantasy Asian beauty was beginning to drive me wild with desire.

As dusk approached, I drove out to the address of the country estate and pulled up to a wrought iron gate at the end of a long driveway. A call box sat on the driver's side of the entrance. I pressed the button and an unfamiliar woman's voice answered.

"Good evening. May I help you?"

"Yes, I have an appointment for this evening's Fantasy Feast."

"May I ask your profile name?"

I liked how they protected my privacy at every stage of the affair. I hadn't had to provide any revealing personal identification information, not even my credit card. Apparently, my profile name would be my pseudonym for the rest of the evening.

"It's Jade," I said. It was such a thrill to vocalize my new name. I could feel myself already getting into character.

"Please come in. A hostess will meet you at the front door."

The gates swung open, and I drove slowly up the long tree-lined driveway toward an enormous floodlit villa. It was a magnificent chateau in the French Renaissance style, clad in pale yellow limestone with tall Palladian windows rising three stories above manicured gardens. It had to be five times the size of a normal home. To my provincial eyes, it looked like the Palace of Versailles.

I parked my car in the designated area and walked toward the large double entrance door. Soft incandescent light shone through the glass sidelights and an overhead crescent window into the gathering dusk. I tapped gently with the brass door knocker and heard the sound of high heels on a tile floor coming toward me from behind the door.

A gorgeous young woman wearing a cat mask opened the door and motioned me inside. She was completely nude except for her skimpy mask and tall stilettos. Her slender, toned legs rose to the perfectly bald 'V' of her pubis, framed by hourglass-shaped hips. Her breasts were full and firm and swayed gently as she moved toward me. I couldn't help but glance downward to take in her breathtaking beauty.

"You must be Jade," she said softly. "Please come in. May I take your coat?"

"Thank you," I practically choked, my mind still swimming in shock.

The young woman stepped behind me and helped me remove my coat, then hung it in the large closet in the entrance foyer. Even just the soft touch of her hands on my fully clothed shoulders put a charge of electricity through me.

"Please follow me," she said. "Our hostess is expecting you."

I followed the nude woman across the expansive open foyer as her heels clicked on the marble floor tiles. My eyes were locked on the perfectly shaped globes of her ass as they flexed and bounced with each forward step. I could barely keep myself erect as my knees weakened beneath me.

The woman escorted me into a large private study with mahogany paneling and leather armchairs.

"May I get you a coffee or glass of wine?"

"A coffee would be fine, thank you," I said, trying my best to sound sophisticated. "Black, with just a bit of sugar."

"A hostess will be with you shortly. Please make yourself comfortable."

The woman exited through a side door, and two minutes later a slightly older woman in her thirties entered carrying a cup of coffee on a platter. She too was completely naked, other than the feathered Mardi Gras mask partially covering her eyes. She placed the platter on a table beside my chair and extended her hand to me.

"It's a pleasure to meet you, Jade."

I recognized the sultry voice immediately. It was the Scarlett Johansson voice from my earlier phone conversation.

She took a seat in the leather chair directly opposite me and crossed her legs, barely concealing her bare vulva resting on the edge of the chair.

"My name's Blair. I just wanted to take a few minutes to ask you a few brief questions before you begin the festivities. Just to clarify expectations and ensure you're comfortable moving forward."

I liked how she didn't call it an interview, though I knew this was part of my final qualification to participate in the event. I was actually glad they didn't take just anyone who walked in off the street and were careful to set expectations before jumping right in.

Blair was a contemporary, roughly my age. We both took care of ourselves and were equally attractive. We might even have passed for sisters, especially cloaked under our masquerade masks. The main difference between us was our hair color—mine was a shimmering brown and hers a silky blond.

Of course, she had the benefit of a superior position by virtue of her role as interviewer. But this didn't stop me from imagining myself entwined with her in lots of less *formal* positions.

Her plump breasts pointed toward me, with dark nipples peering like amber eyes, daring me to make contact. A little lower, the shadow at the apex of her legs just under her thighs beckoned even stronger. It took every ounce of my power to keep my eyes leveled with hers.

Two can play this game, I thought. I decided to have some fun and begin role-playing.

"Ask away," I teased, "I'm an open vessel."

Blair paused briefly to appraise my figure and comportment. I was wearing a tight taupe-colored gabardine skirt, hemmed just above the knee, and a cream-colored silk blouse opened to the third button, revealing ample cleavage and my flawless alabaster skin. I'd intentionally gone braless, partly to put myself in an erotic mood—and partly to display my best assets.

I straightened my back and crossed my right leg over the other slowly. I could feel my nipples swelling as they protruded teasingly in the outline of my flimsy blouse. I was pretty sure I'd pass this part of the test.

Blair cleared her throat.

"That's good to hear," she said. "Actually, that was one of my first questions. How open are you to engaging with others this evening?"

"You mean besides enjoying the *food* and *conversation*?" I let a slight smile cross my lips.

"If the opportunity presents."

"Well, as you suggested on the phone, I'm looking forward to exploring *all* of my senses."

"Wonderful. We wouldn't want you to miss out on the potential to fulfill all of your desires." Blair paused for a moment. "And if some of the contact is—*unexpected*—will you be comfortable engaging?"

The more Blair spoke, the more turned on I got by her sexy voice and subtle nuances of meaning. She was seriously hot, and her sophisticated manner was getting me all the more worked up. I knew exactly what she meant, but I wanted to extend the foreplay a little longer.

"I suppose that depends on what you mean by 'contact', and 'engaging'."

Blair looked me directly in the eyes as her lips curled in a faint smile.

"You understand that the Fantasy Feast experience will engage all your senses, including *touch*? Are you open to being touched, gently and with your full permission of course, at one or more times during the course of the dinner engagement?"

I was pretty clear on the terms of engagement coming in, but I still wanted to confirm a few details.

"On the phone, you said everyone would remain seated at the table until the meal is finished. Only then would we have an opportunity to approach other patrons directly?"

"That's true. But there may be opportunities over the course of the meal for our *own* sensualists to engage you in various pleasurable ways. Are you open to that?"

I paused for a moment. The idea of being 'serviced' while others watched was in fact one of the main attractions for my wanting to come.

"Will I have the ability to control or stop the activities at any time?"

I was backsliding a little in my confident role-playing, but this was not a matter to be ambiguous about. This was my only hard and fast rule when it came to sex. "No" always means no.

"Yes. You'll have a signaling device directly at your place setting and will be able to stop—or start—any of the activities at any time."

Blair paused to ensure I was comfortable with what she'd said.

"Did you have any *other* questions or concerns before you begin your spa preparation?"

There was only one other concern that had crossed my mind. I wasn't quite sure how to put it delicately.

"What precautions have you taken to ensure the...*cleanliness* of the participants and the utensils"? I wasn't sure who, or *what* exactly, would be touching me, but I wanted to be sure everything would at least be sterile and disease-free.

Blair nodded, understanding my meaning.

"That's an excellent question. All of our servers and sensualists receive a weekly medical checkup and blood test for any communicable diseases. Our dinnerware and other paraphernalia is steam-cleaned with organic detergents at 220 degrees-plus water temperatures to ensure absolute sterility."

I could see that Blair was impressed by the type of questions I was asking.

"Of course," she nodded, "we expect *reciprocal* disclosure from our guests. You've already verified your health when you submitted your online profile, but if you have any concerns regarding this matter, now is the time to share."

I breathed a sigh of relief to get this awkward subject out of the way.

"I'm fine, thank you, Blair. I too have received a full check-up and clean bill of health recently."

Blair stood up and smiled.

"In that case, if you're ready to begin the process, I'll take you to our spa where you'll meet with our esthetician, who'll prepare you for the main event. Please follow me as I escort you to your private room."

I followed Blair out of the study and up a long winding staircase. From my vantage point three steps below her, I could see her thighs opening slightly as she lifted each leg, revealing the tantalizing cleft between her cheeks. It might have been my over-active imagination, but I could have sworn I saw her lips glistening in the bright light of the chandelier hanging above the foyer.

I wondered if I would see her again before the evening was over.

5
———

FINGER FOOD

When we got to the top of the stairs, Blair led me into a beautifully appointed private boudoir with ensuite bathroom.

But this was no *ordinary* bathroom. It was a luxury spa with heated white marble floors and countertops. In the middle of the expansive floor rested a linen-covered massage table with a plump pillow at the head. Next to a large window covered with soft sheers sat a large soaking tub filled with steaming water and floating rose petals. A subtle aroma of lemongrass permeated the room as soft music played from the overhead speakers.

"This will be your private suite to use as you please for the next twenty-four hours," Blair said.

"If you'd like to relax with a warm bath or a stimulating shower, please make yourself comfortable. In thirty minutes, your masseuse will arrive to complete your preparation for the main event. If you need anything at all, please feel free to call us on the courtesy phone."

I was amazed how relaxed and utterly nonchalant a naked woman could be in the company of strangers. Before the evening was over, I hoped to achieve a similar state of intrepidness. I wanted to strip off my clothes right there and ask Blair to join me in the tub, but I knew that was against the rules. Instead, I simply smiled and made love to her with my eyes.

"Thank you, Blair. I think a stimulating bath is *just* what my body could use right now. How will I find my way to the dining room?"

"Your attendant will escort you to the dining hall at the appointed hour. I look forward to seeing you then."

So this wasn't to be the last of her *after* all. My heart raced and my pussy pulsed at the thought of seeing her again. Blair turned and left the room, closing the main bedroom door softly behind her.

I took a few minutes to walk about the bedroom and washroom to appraise my surroundings. Everything about the accommodations was first-class. From the high thread count Egyptian cotton sheets on the king-size bed to the cherry-wood furnishings, it felt like a five-star hotel. They even had a large bottle of Evian water and a collection of dark chocolates on the nightstand beside the bed.

I swung open the doors to the large armoire to hang my clothes. A beautiful floral kimono hung on a padded silk hanger. I reached out and caressed the softness of the fabric. Forget one *day*—I'd like to book an entire *week* at this spa!

I disrobed and hung my blouse and skirt in the armoire, then laid my panties on the paper-lined shelf of the top drawer. Normally, I'd be reluctant to place my intimate clothes in a public area, but the paper smelled fresh and looked newly laid.

Now completely naked, I appraised myself in the full-length wardrobe mirror. I looked pretty damn good for a nearly middle-aged woman. My yoga-toned body was tight and curvy in all the right places. My full and natural breasts still sat high and firm on my chest with large brown nipples. Long shapely legs cascaded down from my heart-shaped ass, a small wedge of light showing between my slightly parted thighs.

I'd booked an appointment with my stylist the day before, and my shoulder-length hair rested perfectly straight just above my shoulders. The only thing that needed a slight trim was my pubic bush, which I'd intentionally let grow over the last week in anticipation of the esthetic grooming I knew was yet to come.

I unhooked the kimono from the armoire hanger and carried it to the edge of the bath, where I hung it on a hook next to the window. The water had been pre-heated to the perfect temperature—warm enough to relax my muscles, but not so hot to feel uncomfortable or scalding. I slowly lowered myself onto the oil-covered surface and parted the rose petals as my body submerged into the heavenly ocean.

I immediately felt the tension begin to ebb from my body as I lost myself in the sublime sensation enveloping me. The only sound I could hear was the soft music playing from the surround speakers and the gentle lapping of water against the sides of the tub. I lay my head back against the pillow placed at the top edge of the tub and soon nodded off.

Sometime later, I heard a soft tap on my bedroom door. Not wanting to remove myself just yet from my cocoon of luxury, I called out to answer.

"Yes?"

"It's time for your massage," a woman's voice replied.

"Just one minute please."

I reluctantly stepped out of the bath and quickly toweled

myself dry. I wrapped a large bath sheet around me, re-donned my mask, then opened the bedroom door.

A petite young Asian girl greeted me, wearing a kimono similar to mine and a crimson masquerade mask.

Apparently not *everybody* who works here always walks around stark naked.

The girl was utterly breathtaking. Long jet-black hair cascaded over high cheekbones past her pouty lips with delicate collarbones peeking from the top of her kimono. I could see her breasts and hips outlined by the tightly wrapped kimono and suddenly wished that she too had come to my boudoir naked.

"My name is Jasmine," she said. "I'm your personal masseuse and esthetician. Are you ready for your final preparation?"

Just the thought of this beauty laying her tender hands on me sent a shiver down my spine.

"Definitely," I said. "Please come in. How would you like me to prepare?"

"Come with me, please."

Jasmine led me into the bathroom, where she nonchalantly removed her kimono and hung it behind the bathroom door.

Oh my God.

I didn't think anyone in this place could get more beautiful or sensuous. Jasmine had perfectly shaped B-cup breasts with a thin indentation running down the center of her toned stomach. Like everyone else in this place, her pubis was utterly bald and flawless. She barely looked eighteen and I was just about to ask her age, but she spoke first.

"If you'd like to remove your towel and lay face down on the table, we can get started. May I call you Jade?"

There was something about her confident manner and

tone that belied her youthful appearance. I had no inhibitions whatsoever about displaying myself unclothed to this stranger.

"Yes, thank you, Jasmine." I unhooked my bath sheet and threw it against the side of the tub.

"Would you like me to drape your backside?" Jasmine asked.

"That won't be necessary," I quickly answered.

Jasmine walked over to the vanity counter and picked up two small bottles of oil resting under an orange radiant lamp. She brought them back to the massage table, opened one, and poured the oil into one cupped hand then rubbed her hands together. The scent of lavender wafted toward my nose.

I closed my eyes in anticipation of her touch. I'd had massages before, but nothing as sensuous and stimulating as this. When her hands touched the small of my back, I flinched reflexively from the sexual tension. My heart was beating a hundred miles an hour as I felt the blood coursing through my veins.

Jasmine must have sensed my nervous tension and began pressing her fingers more firmly into my back as she moved them slowly up each side of my spine. The warm oil allowed her hands to glide effortlessly across my skin. She used every surface of her hands to massage my muscles, expertly kneading my skin with her fingers and palm.

I began to relax as my muscles softened and surrendered to her touch. She sensuously massaged every part of my back, shoulders, and neck, applying just the right amount of pressure. Periodically, she would pour more warm oil on my lower back, dipping her hands in it to replenish the silky lubrication against my pliant skin.

Just as the sexual tension began to subside from the

utter relaxation of the massage, Jasmine moved her hands down to my buttocks and began to caress them in soft circular motions. My glutes contracted involuntarily and I unconsciously pressed my mound into the firm padding of the table. Suddenly I was quickly reminded that a gorgeous young woman was caressing my naked body. She cupped each buttock between her hands as she massaged my ass tantalizingly, her little finger sliding slowly into the cleft just above my anus.

Periodically, I'd partially open one of my eyes with my head turned in her direction to look at her gorgeous body. My head was at the same level as her midsection, and my mouth watered as I watched her stomach muscles flex and her hips undulate with each movement of her hands. At times her pussy was almost right beside me and I wanted to reach out and run my own fingers up her soft legs.

I was in total heaven, and getting wetter by the moment. Just when I thought I couldn't stand it anymore, she suddenly moved her hands down to my feet and began massaging her thumbs into my soles.

I'd always loved having my feet massaged, but nobody did it like Jasmine. She cradled my foot and used every part of her hands to massage and knead every surface from my heel to my toes. I didn't want her to stop, but there were *other* parts of my body that were screaming for attention.

As if reading my thoughts, she began moving her hands up toward my calf, using her thumbs to spread the muscle apart. She lingered almost as long on my calf as she had on my foot, rolling the ball of my calf between both of her hands, sliding her slick hands up and down erotically. I couldn't help imagining how she might use those same hands to massage a man's erect cock in a similar manner. My mind wandered again to what pleasures lay in wait for me over dinner.

After shifting her hands to my right leg and giving my other foot and calf similar attention, she placed each hand just behind my knees and began to slowly move them up towards my buttocks. Her thumbs pressed against my inner thighs as she glided tantalizingly close to my apex.

I rolled my legs outward in an invitation to move closer. My legs were parted enough that I was sure she could see my vulva from her vantage point behind me. In my highly aroused state, my lips were engorged and spread apart, revealing my moist and quivering opening.

But as much as I desperately wanted her to, Jasmine never touched me there. She repeatedly slid her hands right up to the edge of my slit, pressing and rotating her thumbs on the fleshy meat of my upper thighs just below my aching pussy. I suppose this was part of her master plan—to tease me mercilessly and inflame my passions so I'd be ready for just about anything at the main event.

It was certainly working. After thirty minutes of Jasmine's ministrations, I was grinding my pussy into the table trying desperately to give my clit some needed direct stimulation.

Just when I thought I couldn't be teased any more tantalizingly, Jasmine opened one of the bottles of warm oil and poured it directly into the crack of my ass. She paused as the fluid flowed down and directly over my parted lips. I almost came from the gentle movement of the warm liquid as it trickled across the folds of my labia, channeled toward the junction where they joined together at my clit. I shuddered in pleasure at the feeling, even if it was only the subtlest of touch.

Jasmine suddenly interrupted my thoughts.

"Would you like to turn over now?"

It was the first time she'd spoken directly to me since the massage started, and it surprised me in my catatonic, pre-orgasmic state. I practically flipped over like a fish out of water, spreading my legs expectantly. Finally, I'd get some relief. Surely, she couldn't leave me hanging like this.

"It's time for your final grooming," she said. "I'll need you to part your legs a bit further to provide full access."

Grooming? I knew this was part of the process, but somehow it didn't seem fair to transition at this precise moment. At least I'd be able to stay on the comfortable massage table instead of the clinical vinyl chairs used by my regular esthetician.

Jasmine walked over to another cabinet by the makeup table and withdrew a leather bag from one of the drawers, then brought it back to the table. She reached into the bag and pulled out a cordless hair trimmer.

"Do you have a preference regarding your appearance?" she asked. "Do you prefer natural, neatly trimmed, or bare?"

I knew she was referring to my pubic hair, which I generally kept neatly trimmed. I'd always thought going fully bald was unnatural and unseemly, catering to men's prurient fantasies of fucking young schoolgirls. But in this situation, it seemed entirely appropriate, like I was stripping away all my camouflage and armor.

If tonight was all about being *watched*, I might as well bare myself in every sense of the word and truly let my inhibitions go. I began to fantasize about rubbing my bare pussy against Jasmine's while she poured warm oil between us. The more work she had to do on me, the more chance I'd have to make this last and hopefully get off.

I didn't hesitate. "Bare, thank you."

"As you wish," she said. "I'll remove the long hairs first with the trimmer, then shave you smooth with a razor."

No *waxing*? This was different. I was relieved to not have to bear the painful and violent trial of having my hairs ripped out en masse. Although shaving down there was always a scary proposition, I felt safe in the capable and practiced hands of this beautiful esthetician.

Jasmine nodded, then flipped a switch on the trimmer. The device buzzed softly as she placed it gently on my mound. I had only a light dusting of fur and it didn't take long for her to remove it with a few short strokes over my pubis. I shuddered as the vibrations penetrated deep into my core. If she had placed the flat head on my clitoris, I would have popped off in a millisecond. Instead, she turned the trimmer face-down and gently swiped the vibrating teeth against the sides of my vulva, sensuously separating my labia with her hands as she moved the device between my legs to trim the hairs on the inside and outside of my labia.

It was an insanely titillating feeling, but just clinical enough to bring me down from my plateau and shift my focus. My mind wandered to the upcoming feast, and I contemplated what surprises lay in wait at the main event. The hostess had suggested there would be 'contact' of some sort during the meal, and I was intrigued as to who and how it would be administered. The idea of being fully bald, cleansed, and thoroughly stimulated going into the event was an incredible rush.

Jasmine continued with the trimmer all the way down my perineum to my anus, barely touching me with the trimmer so as not to pinch any delicate tissues. Apparently, there were no parts of my erogenous zone that would remain untouched, now—and perhaps later.

She turned off the trimmer and placed it at the foot of the table. Then she took a bottle of gel from the bag and spread the gel on her hands. Using both hands, she spread it gently between my legs, starting on my mound all the way down to my rosebud.

My body almost levitated above the table as Jasmine finally laid her hands directly on my clitoris. The gel had a mild stinging quality that added to the stimulating sensation. If this was meant to excite my follicles in preparation for the shave, it wasn't the *only* feature of my anatomy that it made erect. I could feel the hood of my clitoris retract as my button filled with blood and began to push outward. Suddenly, I was fully stimulated again and lusting for Jasmine's touch. I fantasized about her bending down and taking my swollen nub between her puffy lips and letting me come in her mouth.

Unfortunately, my satisfaction would have to wait a little longer. Instead, Jasmine reached into her bag and pulled out a straight-edge razor. In anyone else's hands, it might look threatening, especially in my prostrated and vulnerable position. But something about the way she delicately and sensuously opened the jackknifed tool instantly evaporated my fears. I could see how this type of razor would in fact give her better control safely cutting my stubs instead of the usual ladies' plastic razor.

With her right hand, Jasmine gently laid the razor on its flat edge at the top of my mound, while she gently pulled my skin upwards with her other hand. Then she slowly turned the sharp edge perpendicular to my skin and began softly scraping the razor downwards. I could hear the bristling sound as the razor edge removed my nubs right down to the follicles. She repeated the pattern in one-inch-wide swipes on one side then the other of my pubis, being ever-so-careful to stop just where my clitoris lay quivering in a mixture of fear and excitement. There was something about the utter vulnerability of the procedure that made it the most erotic experience I'd ever had.

Jasmine used the same deft touch as she moved down my vulva and perineum, scraping the vestiges of stray hairs away with gentle swipes of the long blade, while sensuously separating my folds and flesh with her other hand. She took extra time and care around my anus and clit, using the gentlest and slowest motion I've ever felt someone apply to my body. The combination of fright and titillation as she probed my most sensitive body parts created a river of sensuous fluids running down my vulva. By this time, no shaving gel was necessary to provide a smooth gliding surface for the knife.

When she was finished, Jasmine retrieved a fresh wash towel from beside the sink and held it under the warm water faucet then twisted the excess water into the basin. She returned to the table and placed it over my splayed legs then gently cleansed the excess moisture and remaining shaving gel with gentle massaging movements of her hands. The warm, moist towel felt exquisite against my newly shaved skin. Jasmine's hands now felt comforting between my legs rather than erotic.

She had taken me on an incredibly sensuous erotic arc, right to the edge of ecstasy and back, to a quiet relaxed place. I exhaled fully and completely for the first time in almost an hour.

Jasmine removed the towel from between my legs and held up a large hand mirror at a forty-five-degree angle toward me.

"What do you think?" she asked.

I tilted my head up and studied her masterpiece. Far

from the usual red and swollen vulva that I typically experienced after the violent waxing with my regular esthetician, I'd never seen my pussy look so beautiful. Utterly bereft of any hair, my entire perineum from my pubic mound to my anus was totally bald, pink—and gorgeous. I just stared at my beautiful pussy, utterly transfixed by the transformation.

"You have to *feel* it to really appreciate how beautiful you are," Jasmine purred.

I moved my right hand down, running my fingers along the edges of my pussy. I gasped from a feeling I'd never felt before. It felt smooth as silk: no bumps or blemishes or cuts or bruises. It was almost as if I was feeling somebody *else*— somebody I'd never felt before. I couldn't stop my left hand joining the other in rubbing and caressing my sensitive organs.

Jasmine lowered the mirror and smiled at me as I felt the moisture begin to accumulate between my legs again.

"It's almost time for your dinner appointment," she said. "Why don't you save the best for last? I think you'll find plenty of ways to satisfy your appetite over the next couple of hours."

She lifted my kimono from the hook at the edge of the bathtub and held it open for me.

"I'll escort you downstairs now if you're ready. All you need to bring is your kimono and slippers—and your mask of course."

I sat up slowly and stepped off the massage table. Turning around, I held my arms out as Jasmine lifted one arm of the silk robe onto me then the other. Then she turned around to face me, wrapped the silk tie around me, and tied a single bow over my belly button. She retrieved my matching silk slippers and knelt down on one knee to gently lift my feet one at a time and place them softly inside. It took every ounce of my power not to grab her head and pull it into my pulsating pussy.

Jasmine stood up gracefully and smiled into my eyes.

"If you'll follow me, I'll escort you now to the fantasy feast."

She didn't even bother putting her own robe on. Her tight little ass barely jiggled as she stepped smartly ahead of me. I wasn't sure if I'd have a chance to feel Jasmine's touch again before the evening was over, but for now I was in total bliss ogling her petite, curvaceous figure from behind.

6

MAIN COURSE

I followed Jasmine down the circular stairs, across the marble-tiled foyer, past an open kitchen where a group of chefs wearing white hats were busy cooking, to a closed set of French doors. Jasmine paused, opened the doors and motioned me inside. I walked into a palatial dining room with a large table seating eight people, all wearing robes and masquerade masks.

The table was covered in a large white linen cloth extending down to the floor. The place settings were beautifully decorated with crystal wine goblets, polished silverware, and gold-embossed dinner plates. At the head of every place setting was a folded tent card with each person's first name and a little silver bell.

The entire scene was surreal. As I followed Jasmine toward the one remaining unoccupied seat at the table, everyone watched me. There was an even mix of men and women appearing to be in their twenties and thirties and of mixed ethnicity, just as my profile preferences had requested. And all of them were beautiful. Some smiled at me as I approached the table.

Jasmine pulled out the empty chair and motioned for me to have a seat. I noticed the chair had a hollow opening in the middle and front section of the seat cushion, shaped almost like a toilet seat. On the back of the chair was a small wooden hook. Otherwise, the chairs were tastefully detailed in full upholstery with high backs and armrests. I sat tentatively down onto the chair and found it surprisingly comfortable. Jasmine exited the room and closed the French doors quietly behind her.

"It looks like we're all here," the woman sitting at the head of the table announced. It was Blair from my interview. She had replaced her feathered mask with a Venetian-style mask and was wearing a robe, but I recognized her unmistakable voice immediately.

"My name is Blair," she said. "I'll be your hostess for the evening. If there's anything you desire at any time, please don't hesitate to ask. We want you to feel comfortable, stimulated, and uplifted throughout the course of our fantasy feast. To that end, may I suggest we begin by disrobing, as a way of releasing our inhibitions and opening ourselves to a fully liberating experience? I'll be the first. If you'd rather keep your robe on for now, that's fine too."

Blair stood up and slowly removed her robe, then hung it on the hook on the back of her chair. She paused for a moment before she sat down to allow everyone to take in her breathtaking beauty. Her plump natural breasts swayed delicately as she turned to face the guests on each side of the table. She was an exquisite specimen of feminine beauty and everyone around the table, men and women alike, were staring just as I was. I was disappointed when she sat down. I could have soaked up her beauty all night long.

"Who else would like to reveal their full beauty for the rest of us to enjoy?" she said.

Blair turned and looked suggestively at the male guest to her immediate right. His place card read Isiah. He paused, momentarily taken aback. But after a few seconds, he also stood and confidently removed his robe then turned and placed it on the hook behind his chair. As he twisted his torso, his tight muscular buttocks flexed to balance his weight. When he turned around, he paused briefly in full frontal view before sitting down. Not everybody was quite as comfortable as Blair getting naked in front of a room full of strangers.

Nonetheless, I saw enough to gain an appreciation of Isiah's toned physique. An African-American with light brown skin, chiseled pecs and six-pack abs descending to a neatly trimmed pubic area, his half-erect circumcised member betrayed his obvious excitement. Already at least six inches long in a semi-flaccid state, I could only imagine how large he might be fully aroused and erect. As he lowered himself onto his chair holding the armrests, his well-toned arm muscles flexed in a light sheen of perspiration.

He wasn't the *only* one already beginning to lubricate this evening.

Everyone around the table looked towards Blair. You could hear a pin drop from the nervous and excited tension in the room. Blair peered at the pretty redheaded woman seated next to Isiah and smiled. The redhead's place card read Venus. Where do these people come up with their profile names?

Perhaps she was trying to overcompensate for her shyness. Her eyes widened in a mix of fear and nervousness. She paused, looking at Blair uncertainly. Then she took a deep breath, quickly stood up and removed her robe, and hung it behind her chair. She sat back down immediately, her back arched a few inches away from the backrest with a ramrod straight spine. Her perky breasts rested firmly on her chest with pinched nipples betraying her excitement.

Her face was expressionless as she stared straight ahead, afraid to make eye contact with anyone in her fully exposed state. It was obvious this was the first time she'd done anything like this, probably coming from an upper-class repressive home, like myself. It was kind of comforting to know that I wasn't the only relatively inexperienced one among the group.

One by one, everyone around the table removed their robes, sitting stark naked except for their masks. The men seemed more comfortable disrobing than the women. The next woman awkwardly removed her robe while still seated, apparently not ready to reveal her most intimate parts to the group just yet. The last woman simply parted the top portion of her robe, revealing half of her bare bosom. I was glad that Blair didn't make anyone feel uncomfortable or set any expectations as the disrobing ritual continued around the table. She simply smiled and acknowledged each person as they revealed as much as they wanted.

The four women and four men were evenly spaced around the oversize table in alternating sexes. Just as I had specified, everyone was young, beautiful, and of mixed heritage. Besides Isiah, there was a Latino man who looked like a young Benicio Del Toro, a dark-haired Patrick Dempsey lookalike, and a thick blond-haired hunk who reminded me of his McSteamy counterpart on the TV show Grey's Anatomy. All the men were tall, fit—and gorgeous. It was like my own *Chippendale* show, and I stared shamelessly at the strong toned torsos of the men sitting majestically around the table.

In addition to the shy redhead Venus, the women were

represented by a pretty young Asian woman who reminded me a bit of Jasmine, a dark exotic black woman who looked like Naomi Campbell, myself—and of course, Blair. As with the men, all the women were young, attractive, and perfectly toned. It was obvious that this was a discriminating club that catered to the most beautiful and uninhibited.

When it became *my* turn to disrobe, I hesitated briefly, feeling slightly inadequate amongst this stunning group of Adonises and Lorelei. Blair simply smiled at me and nodded. I paused for a second, then stood confidently, pulling my kimono away in a flourish. My plump breasts bounced firmly as I bent over and hooked my robe behind my chair. The idea of displaying my newly sculpted nude body to a group of strangers was a huge turn-on, and I hesitated for a few seconds before sitting down to let everyone have a good look.

I could feel the electricity in the room as everyone looked around the table and took in the sights and sounds and scents. A distinct womanly perfume permeated the room as an obvious state of arousal began to build among the dinner patrons. My vulva twitched as I felt the cool movement of air against my genitals in the opening of my seat cushion.

Knowing everyone else was feeling the same thing and was equally exposed under the tablecloth was incredibly stimulating. My pussy throbbed and moistened as I imagined the men growing hard and the women getting wet looking at me and the others. I wasn't sure what was going to happen next, but this was definitely the most titillating experience I had so far, and the evening had barely started.

Blair was the first to break the tension as a door swung open and two pretty waitresses began filling our champagne glasses with bubbly.

"I'm glad everyone has made themselves comfortable," she said. "We will begin serving our first courses shortly. Please enjoy our services and allow all your senses to be stimulated. Don't be alarmed if you experience something new at one or more times during the dinner service. The only rule we ask you to honor is that you keep your hands in plain sight at all times. And remember, all you have to do is ring this little bell at your place setting if you feel uncomfortable and wish to stop the services at any time."

Blair picked up the silver bell at the head of her place setting and tinkled it teasingly. Then she lifted her champagne glass in a toast and everyone followed her lead.

"To unleashing inhibitions, and experiencing transcendence!"

Everyone took a deep swig of their champagne and smiled. They knew the main event was about to begin. The pretty waitresses returned carrying silver platters and placed bowls of gazpacho in front of each dinner guest. Over the next hour or so, Blair facilitated polite chit-chat around the table, referring to everyone by their first name only. Occasionally, one or more guests engaged each other directly in conversation, but always over safe subjects. Whether it was the awkward feeling of being utterly naked or trepidation over what was coming next, everybody seemed on edge.

I was almost disappointed when I picked up my dessert spoon and cut into my crème brulée. So far, it had been a fairly uneventful dinner, except for the obvious staring among the dinner patrons at each other's nude torsos.

Then, for the first time over the course of the dinner event, Blair became conspicuously quiet. Everyone ate their dessert silently, glancing nervously at each other around the table. None of us were still entirely comfortable engaging each other in direct conversation without Blair's facilitation.

Suddenly, the redheaded girl gasped and jerked in her chair. Her right hand reflexively reached out to the bell and she considered shaking it as she glanced uncertainly in Blair's direction. Blair simply smiled and nodded at her. Whatever was going on at Venus's seat, Blair was apparently fully aware and giving her silent encouragement to continue.

Venus's breathing became more labored and she set her fork down beside her chocolate torte to steady herself. She moved her hands to her chair armrests and closed her eyes. It was obvious that something was going on below our line of sight as she began squirming seductively in her chair. Her lips parted and she moaned softly. She sank lower in her chair as it was apparent her legs were spreading apart.

Who, or what, was ministering to her under the table obviously was having the desired effect. My pussy began dripping down the crack of my ass as I watched Venus enjoying herself, imagining what was being done to her under the table. Her hands stayed above the table, so she apparently didn't need any help getting satisfaction.

Suddenly, Venus gasped, locking eyes on me. She was moving rhythmically now in her seat, thrusting her hips in a violent motion as her passion progressively rose. By now, *everyone* around the table had placed their utensils down and was watching the beautiful redhead enjoy her erotic encounter.

I wanted desperately to reach down and touch myself as Venus looked at me through glistening eyes with lust and abandon. I began to move in synchronicity with her, rotating my hips to her rhythm, trying to find the edge of my seat to rub against my twitching clit. Venus's cheeks flushed and the pale skin on her upper chest reddened as her breasts heaved with the movement of her hips. Whatever was happening to her under the table, I wanted some of that.

By this point, Venus's inhibitions had completely evaporated as she was lost in the moment. As her passion rose and she moved closer to climax, she moaned louder and more lustfully. Whimpering in ecstasy, her release came like a volcano as she screamed and grunted like a wild animal with a long and powerful orgasm. Her chest heaved in rhythmic spasms as each wave of passion rolled over her. When she was finally spent, she slumped in her chair and closed her eyes in utter satiation.

Everyone looked at one another around the table in total shock and excitement. Nobody said a word, but we were all thinking the same thing. This had been the most erotic experience any of us had ever witnessed, and each of us was dripping and throbbing in anticipation of receiving similar treatment.

Unsure exactly how to respond, I simply picked up my fork and resumed eating my dessert. Others around the table followed suit. Blair smiled at Venus when she finally regained her composure and sat back up in her chair.

"Did you enjoy your *dessert*, Venus?"

"It was exquisite," Venus panted.

Everyone around the table smiled. For another minute or so, all I could hear was the sound of silverware tinkling against dessert dishes and Venus's contented sighs.

But it didn't take long before *Isiah* started squirming in his seat also. Suddenly, he slammed his palms on the table and jerked his body. It was obviously his turn to be serviced under the table. There was something incredibly erotic about not being able to use your own hands and simply abandon yourself to the ministrations of some unknown stranger or strangers. The long skirt of the linen tablecloth obscured any direct sightlines—even *he* couldn't know if it was a man or woman massaging his erogenous zones.

Whoever, or whatever it was, he was obviously enjoying it. His eyes glazed over and his arm muscles tensed as he held the armrests of his chair to secure himself. The six-pack muscles in his abdomen flexed as he began to thrust his hips rhythmically. My mind was going crazy imagining what was being done to him. I could hear a slapping noise mixed with a wet sound. Whether it was a mouth or a set of hands on his cock, it was difficult to tell. Something told me at this particular moment Isiah didn't care.

His breathing was becoming more ragged and his mouth was fully open now, and I could tell he was nearing the point of no return. Suddenly, his body lurched and he let out a guttural moan that indicated something new was happening. He hadn't come yet though, since his breathing was still rapid and building. What could they be doing to him under the table? I wondered if there might be more than one person servicing him. There certainly was enough room under the large table to accommodate multiple sensualists.

My pussy was throbbing with excitement as I became more conscious of the hole in my chair. My entire vulva was exposed as I felt the movement of air from the activity under the table. Isiah was now bouncing up and down in his chair in complete abandon. I'd read about how some erotic masseuses could stimulate a man's prostate by inserting a finger or dildo in his ass—maybe this is what he was experiencing.

Whatever it was, it didn't take long for the procedure to have its desired effect. Isiah let out a long guttural moan and he thrust his hips upward in one last jerk as he threw his head back. He held the armrests tightly in an epileptic spasm that seemed to last thirty seconds, his head and chest jerking in synchronicity with the orgasmic contractions he was experiencing. All I could think about was how much I wanted that thick cock buried in my aching pussy right now. I was dying for relief, having never been stimulated so intensely for so long. Even Jasmine's erotic massage hadn't gotten me this worked up.

I was desperately hoping it would be my turn next, but it was not to be. In fact, I would have to wait until the very end for my turn. One by one, each guest received personal treatment under the table while everyone watched in wonder and unrequited lust. Some took only a few minutes to reach orgasm while others took a little longer. Nobody held out for more than fifteen minutes or so. The turn-on of having eight strangers watching them as they had their erogenous zones stimulated, together with the mystery of not knowing what to expect under the table, was simply impossible to resist. Everybody eventually experienced a strong and explosive orgasm.

Some remained fairly motionless in their chairs as they were being serviced, while others thrashed and hopped about in their seats. It seemed as if some patrons were receiving oral stimulation, while others were being literally fucked under the table—though it was hard to imagine how that could be accomplished in the tight spaces under each chair.

I particularly enjoyed watching the other *women* being serviced. Within a minute or so after beginning their massages, the once demure ladies had thrown open their robes and flung them on the floor to provide easier viewing —and access—to their entire body. I loved watching as their breasts swayed and their skin progressively flushed as their passion mounted and crested. Beyond their telltale cries of ecstasy, I could always tell when they reached orgasm by how the skin on their chest suddenly darkened, then slowly faded along with the tumescence of their engorged nipples.

This Fantasy Feast was definitely on to something. It was true that being able to focus on every sensation in this way, unencumbered by the needs of an active sexual partner, was far more erotic and liberating than straight sex. In our detached and voyeuristic seating positions, all of our *other* sensations could be super-stimulated.

I could literally *smell* the bodily fluids and scented oils flowing from every person. I could see every nuanced movement and expression in their faces as they enjoyed their erotic journey. And of course, I could *hear* their telltale moans of ecstasy, recognizing whenever something changed under the table. Even my sense of *taste* was stimulated from the mouthwatering flavors and textures of each meal course laid out at my place setting.

Of course, the *best* sensation—touch—would have to wait. Which made it all the more tantalizing and enjoyable when it finally happened.

When the last guest before me had finally come down from her high, the anticipation was almost killing me. I was burning with desire like never before. I hoped that I might be able to make my turn last a little longer; I wanted to savor every pleasurable moment. But I knew it would be almost impossible to make it last very long with so much pent-up tension. I glanced at Blair and she simply gave me a knowing smile as if to say: 'just lose yourself in the moment and let it happen.'

I felt some movement under the table in the vicinity of my chair. I parted my legs to invite whoever was there to do as they pleased. Was it too much to hope for my beautiful masseuse Jasmine to finish what she started? She had left me with a cryptic smile. I never actually saw anyone go under or emerge from under the table the whole time. Maybe there was some kind of trap door in the floor to permit easy access to each guest's open chair? It didn't really matter, of course. The whole mystery of who was under the table administering to me simply added to the excitement and eroticism of the moment.

Then the mystery suddenly became clearer. A pair of petite hands began caressing my thighs. The touch was familiar. The motion of the hands, the subtle pressure of the fingertips, the way they floated upward toward my vulva was undeniable. This had to be Jasmine! I spread my legs far apart, fully exposing my pussy, practically *begging* her to fuck me. Or suck me. Or do whatever she pleased with me. I was totally at her mercy, and she knew it.

But she was in no hurry. As with my previous massage, she teased and caressed my thighs with the lightest touch of her fingertips, stroking them up and down my inner thighs. I wanted to cry out "fuck me, Jasmine!"

I could feel her move closer to me as her torso spread my legs further apart. Her hands shifted to the sides of my hips and I felt something touch my vulva. It was soft and round and firm, and it was rubbing softly up and down against my wet twat.

It was her breast! Her gorgeous, perfect, plump, natural breast. She was tribbing me with her breast! My gushing juices coated her skin with a natural lubricant as she pushed up and slid against me. I swear I could feel her erect nipple penetrate me as she thrust rhythmically against me. The combination of the fucking action with the stimulation of her nipple against my clit could easily have brought me to orgasm in less than a minute, but this was obviously not the way she wanted to finish me.

She backed away slowly and I felt her long hair move down lower on my belly and thighs. She began kissing my bald mound that she had so perfectly groomed earlier. I was in utter heaven as I closed my eyes and lost myself in the reality of being kissed by this beauty.

Her hands slowly moved from my hips and began exploring the inside of my thighs as her kisses moved lower and lower toward my nerve center. She kissed around and above and on top of my clit, coming ever so close, but never quite touching me directly. This wasn't like so many fumbling men I'd had who couldn't find my clit for the life of them. This was an expert sensualist who knew exactly how—and where—to tease and please me.

When her lips finally landed on my clit, I almost leaped out of my chair. She surrounded my swollen nub with her full mouth and pursed her lips. The idea of being sucked off by this gorgeous vixen was too much. I groaned uncontrollably and spasmed a mini-orgasm.

But this was only the beginning. Jasmine was obviously far too experienced and practiced to let me off so quickly and so lightly. With my clit still embedded within her lips, she extended her tongue and began swirling it in slow and sensuous movements along the shaft and underside.

Meanwhile, her lips bobbed softly up and down my swollen shaft. If this is what it's like for a man to get a blowjob, I can see why some of the other guests were being driven crazy earlier. Had they gotten similar treatment from Jasmine, or from someone else?

It didn't matter, because for now at least, Jasmine was all mine. I desperately wanted to move my hands under the table and hold her beautiful head while she licked me. I wanted to let her know how much I was enjoying her caresses and feel her soft brown hair flowing in my hands.

My passion rose inexorably as I tried to hold off coming. I wanted to savor this moment as long as I could. This was the first time I'd been intimate with a woman, and I wanted to savor it as long as I could.

Just when I thought it couldn't get any more intense, I felt Jasmine's right hand move to my opening, and she slowly inserted three fingers deep into my vagina. God, I had desperately needed to be fucked, and now this divine creature was answering my prayers.

She began thrusting firmly as she continued sucking and licking my clitoris in a way no one had ever done before. Then she curled her fingers upward and began stroking my G-spot in a come-hither motion that took me to an entirely new level.

I was writhing and thrusting in my chair now, taking everything Jasmine was giving me. I pushed down in my chair wanting more. I wanted my pussy filled up and fucked while I fucked her beautiful mouth with my burning pussy. As if sensing my need, Jasmine inserted her fourth finger inside me and pushed her hand further up inside. I was bucking wildly now and pushing harder and harder against her hand and her mouth. She pressed further until I felt the knuckles of her petite hand slide all the way inside me. She was fucking me with her whole fist!

I threw my head back and grunted like a wild boar. I no longer wanted her gentle touch. I wanted her to ram her fist into me and suck on my swollen button while I flooded her mouth with my erotic juices. I could feel my orgasm building, but I fought it. This was too good. I just wanted another minute in symbiotic union with this beautiful woman.

Jasmine must have sensed what I was up to, because

what she did next sent me over the edge. She reached underneath me with her other hand, now thoroughly oiled with my juices running down my legs, and began circling my anus with her middle finger. This was something else I'd never experienced. Far from being dirty or disgusting, it raised my passion to an entirely new level.

I could tell from Jasmine's delicate touching of my rosebud that she wasn't sure if I wanted to be touched there, but I soon answered her question. I pushed my ass down hard in my chair, pushing the tip of her finger into my opening. Sensing my newfound inhibition, Jasmine slowly worked her finger deeper into my rosebud until it was just past the second knuckle.

My Gawd! The feeling of being fucked on two ends, with my clitoris being sucked and flicked was simply too much. My orgasm washed over me like a tidal wave. I screamed Jasmine's name at the top of my lungs while I pushed my entire vulva as hard as I could into her face, fist, and finger. I could feel the gush of my juices exploding all over her pretty face as I squirted one after another jet of cum into her waiting mouth. My orgasm must have lasted a full minute as I had one hard contraction after another. I could actually feel my pussy and anus clamping down on Jasmine with each contraction.

As my contractions finally began to subside and eventually stop, Jasmine remained perfectly still with my clit still twitching in her mouth, her hands in my most private parts. When my breathing returned to normal and I slumped in my chair, she slowly pulled her hand and fingers from within me. It was the most delicate and intimate thing I had ever experienced. I could sense Jasmine's connection to me, as if she were saying how she enjoyed the experience almost as much as I had.

I never felt so cherished and uplifted in my entire life. I wanted to kiss her and taste my juices in her mouth while I reciprocated with my own delicate touch. I was already thinking about how I'd like to use my private boudoir for the rest of the night...

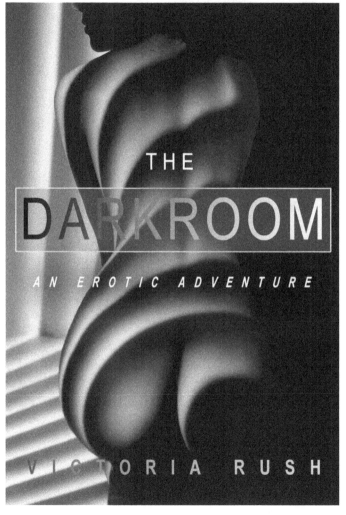

Everything's sexier in the dark...

NAKED
YOGA

AN EROTIC ADVENTURE

VICTORIA RUSH

Mula Bandha is for lovers...

NUDE CRUISE

AN EROTIC ADVENTURE

VICTORIA RUSH

Some people get wet on a cruise for different reasons...

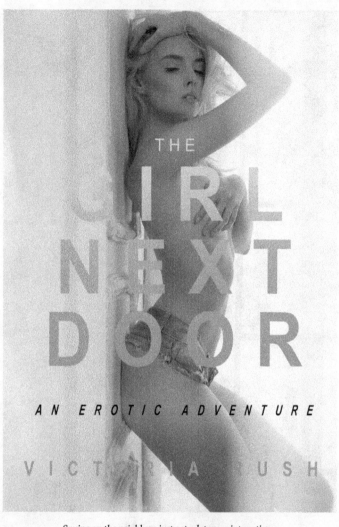

THE
GIRL
NEXT
DOOR

AN EROTIC ADVENTURE

VICTORIA RUSH

Spying on the neighbors just got a lot more interesting...

5 THE SUBWAY AFFAIR
4 NUDE CRUISE
3 NAKED YOGA
2 THE DARK ROOM
1 THE DINNER PARTY

EROTIC ADVENTURES
BOOKS 1-5

Books 1 -5 in the bestselling series - 60% off

THE DARK ROOM - PREVIEW
PEOPLE IN GLASS HOUSES

A li gently clasped my hand and escorted me to the first glass-enclosed cube. It was much larger than it appeared from the other side of the room, measuring roughly twenty feet square on each side, and ten feet tall. Inside the floor-to-ceiling glass panels, I could see the familiar movement of furtive figures illuminated under the kaleidoscopic light. The rest of the room was pitch black, so the only things illuminated by the projecting light were the moving bodies.

I moved closer to the glass, captivated by the swirling light effects and soft music. This wasn't some cheesy strip club with pounding music and bright lights illuminating a gaudy stage. The soft instrumental music combined with the gorgeous light effects projected a feeling of real class. My eyes widened as I watched the naked participants move around inside the room.

Just as in the video, they were swaying their bodies and caressing each other. But there was something different this time. Their hands and bodies were no longer touching each other with fleeting, artificial gestures. This time, they *lingered*—and *probed*—one another. Their action looked *purposeful*, not like the play acting in the video. Near the front of the glass, two women were locked in a tight embrace, kissing passionately and grinding their hips together in familiar motion. I could see their buttock muscles tighten and relax as they rubbed their mounds together under the swirling light.

My eyes raced around the inside of the enclosure as I took it all in. In the far corner of the cube, I could see some neon piping tracing the outline of a large sofa. I squinted my eyes to decipher an unusual commingled figure moving in a different way as the geometric lights swept over a mass of tangled arms and legs. At first, it looked like a single person doing some kind of yoga movement, with her leg over her shoulder. But as I looked more closely, I could see that the raised leg belonged to woman lying on the sofa with her legs splayed apart. Another woman was resting on her knees, squatting between the prone woman's legs, rubbing their vulvas together, fucking her with rapid swings of her hips, while she clasped the prone woman's elevated leg tightly against her breasts.

I gasped audibly and slumped over, unconsciously mimicking the movement of the woman on top.

"Shall I leave you now to enjoy the show?' Ali said, somewhere to my side.

I'd completely forgotten she was still there. I turned and saw her familiar outline flashing beside me under the white strobe light.

"Yes, I'll be fine now," I said, catching my breath, trying to sound composed.

"Wonderful," she said. "You're welcome to remain outside the rooms and watch as long as your session is booked, or enter your allotted rooms at your leisure. The entrance to the dark rooms is via the doctor's office, who'll validate your blood report and conduct a brief external exam. Remember that if you need help at any time, all you have to do is press the button on the side of your bracelet. I hope you enjoy your stay and that we'll see you again soon. Bye for now."

It was strange watching her talk as the white light flashed over her face. I could see her lips open and close in delayed jerky movements that didn't synchronize with her speech. It was a bit disconcerting, and nothing like the flowing movement of the light projected inside the dark room, but it was sexy and mysterious in its own way. Just as she and Sara had promised, it was impossible to recognize her face through the intermittent flashes.

"Thank you, Ali," I said. "I'll let you know if I need anything."

I was glad to see her leave, because my pussy was pounding and my crotch was soaked from watching the action in the cube. As soon as she closed the door leading to the stairs behind her, I unclasped the top button of my jeans and thrust my hand under my panties. My fingers immediately found my opening and I inserted three fingers as far as they'd go while I rubbed my palm against my aching clit. It couldn't have taken more than ten seconds for me to cum hard in my jeans as I watched the women scissoring on the couch in the dark room.

It was difficult to see the expressions on their faces under the shifting light, but I could see the mouth of the woman on top open as her movements became increasingly frenetic. Then she suddenly stopped and arched her back as she pulled her partner's elevated leg against her torso and spasmed her body in obvious climax. I longed to be in the room with them, feeling what they were feeling and listening to their moans of ecstasy as their love juices washed over one another.

After I came down from my orgasm, I suddenly became aware that I wasn't the only one standing outside the cube watching what was going on inside. I noticed another figure standing about five feet to my side and I glanced in her direction. The flashing light showed just enough to reveal a pretty woman with long hair and high cheekbones. Although I'd never recognize her in the plain light of day, her full lips and gently sloping jawline betrayed her beauty. I glanced down at her body, and noticed the bulge of her full breasts in her blouse and the curvature of her hips and ass in her tight jeans.

I blushed in the dark thinking that she might have noticed me rubbing myself in the dark like some kind of creepy flasher. But she just looked at me and smiled.

"Pretty hot, huh?" she said, in a soft, sexy voice.

"Yeah," was all I could manage to pant.

"Are you going in?" she asked, matter-of-factly.

"Definitely," I said.

"Perhaps I'll see you in a few minutes then. I'm going to watch for a little longer to get my nerve up."

"Enjoy," I said, returning her smile. I imagined her getting turned on just as I did watching the action in the cube. Sara was right—it was almost as much fun watching the action as participating in it. But I was eager to feel the touch of another woman and experience the hypnotic light effects first hand.

Those aren't the only body parts I'll be using, I thought, as I headed toward the examining room...

Read More

ABOUT THE AUTHOR

If you would like to receive notification of new book(s) in Jade's Erotic Adventures, follow me at http://bookbub.com/authors/victoria-rush.

If you have a moment, please post a brief review on my Amazon book page at viewbook.at/tdp . Even just a couple of sentences will help other readers find and enjoy this book as much as you hopefully did.

Follow, share, like, and comment at:

www.facebook.com/authorvictoriarush
www.pinterest.com/authorvictoriarush
www.twitter.com/authorvictoriarush
authorvictoriarush@outlook.com

Hope to see you again soon!

Printed in the USA
CPSIA information can be obtained
at www.ICGtesting.com
LVHW041341221123
764619LV00004B/308

9 781777 389109